Bunny Braves the Day

A First-Day-of-School Story

Suzanne Bloom

BOYDS MILLS PRESS
AN IMPRINT OF BOYDS MILLS & KANE
New York

Boyds Mills Press
An Imprint of Boyds Mills & Kane
boydsmillspress.com
Printed in China

ISBN: 978-1-68437-812-8
Library of Congress Control Number: 2019939422

First edition
10 9 8 7 6 5 4 3 2 1

The text is set in Neutraface Text.
The illustrations are done in watercolor, pencil, and colored pencil.

For Kai and Isa who've braved the day

and to our firsts—Ava, Henry & Sojourner

Up and at 'em, Bunny Lump.

I'm not going.

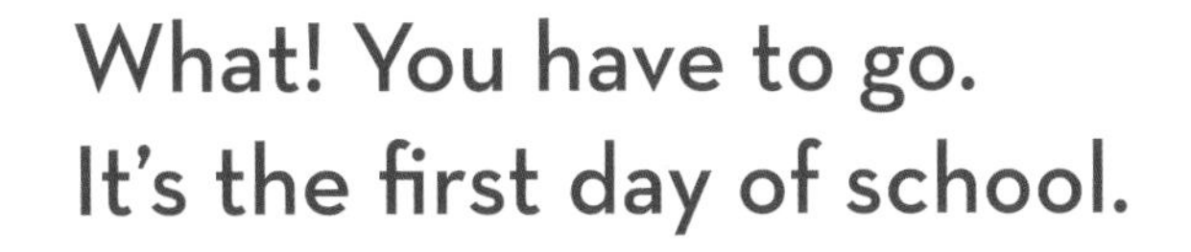

What! You have to go.
It's the first day of school.

No I don't.
I'm hibernating.

Why?

I’m too tired.
I’m not ready.
I won’t know anybody.

What if no one likes me?

Are you nervous?
I was nervous so I put Alli in my pocket.

Did it help?

Sort of.
Then I made friends with Ava.

Maybe I'll wear
my tiger tail.

Good look.
Get dressed.

I can’t.

Why not?

I can’t find my underpants.

My socks are too short.

My shorts are too long.

I can’t even tie my shoes!

You’ve got the jitters.
When I had the jitters, I wore my slip-on glitter shoes.

Did it help?

Pretty much.

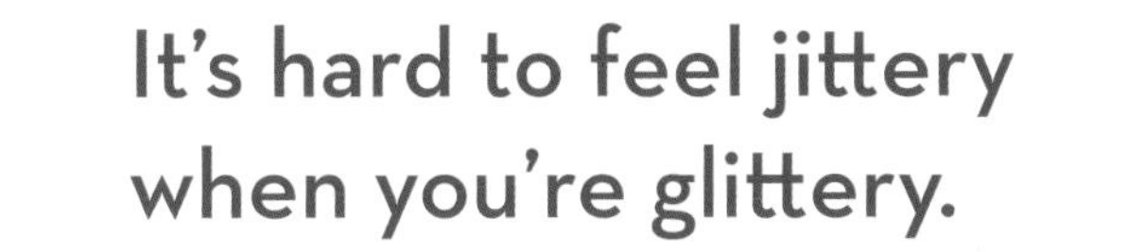

It’s hard to feel jittery
when you’re glittery.

Maybe I’ll wear
my super shirt.

Good choice.
Let’s get breakfast.

Nope. Nopity-nope nope nope.

I might have a cold.
I'm probably contagious.

I feel like a big giant frog is flip-flopping in my belly.
It's trying to hop up my throat.
And what if it comes out!

So I better not go . . .

Because I don't even know how to read!

THE BUS FOR US
Suzanne Bloom
BUS STOP

Oh, Bunny.

Sometimes you just feel like crying
before you feel like trying.

You'll find a friend.
Not all shoes use laces.
And teachers love to teach reading.
It's what they live for.

Besides, you know lots of things.

You know how to make Mom smile.
You can dance like a happy dragon.
Your drawings are fabuloso.

And best of all,
you're curious.
You like to
learn new things.

Okay.
I'm ready. Except for
one more thing.
Mom will miss me.

Mom will be at work all day.
Remember?

I think she might need
my tiger tail.

You're a brave bunny.
You can do this.

11